I Can Be Anything!

I CAN BE A POLICE OFFICER

By Audrey Charles

Please visit our website, www.garethstevens.com. For a free color catalog of all our high-quality books, call toll free 1-800-542-2595 or fax 1-877-542-2596.

Cataloging-in-Publication Data

Names: Charles, Audrey.
Title: I can be a police officer / Audrey Charles.
Description: New York : Gareth Stevens Publishing, 2018. | Series: I can be anything! | Includes index.
Identifiers: ISBN 9781482463255 (pbk.) | ISBN 9781482463279 (library bound) | ISBN 9781482463262 (6 pack)
Subjects: LCSH: Police–Juvenile literature. | Police–Vocational guidance–Juvenile literature.
Classification: LCC HV7922.C43 2018 | DDC 363.2'3–dc23

First Edition

Published in 2018 by
Gareth Stevens Publishing
111 East 14th Street, Suite 349
New York, NY 10003

Editor: Therese Shea
Designer: Sarah Liddell

Photo credits: Cover, p. 1 (kid) glenda/Shutterstock.com; cover, p. 1 (background) Brad Sauter/Shutterstock.com; pp. 5, 19, 24 (officer) John Roman Images/Shutterstock.com; p. 7 asiseeit/E+/Getty Images; p. 9 Zoran Karapancev/Shutterstock.com; p. 11 ZoranOrcik/Shutterstock.com; p. 13 bikeriderlondon/Shutterstock.com; p. 15 OgnjenO/Shutterstock.com; p. 17 Mark Daffey/Getty Images; pp. 21, 24 (motorcycle) B Christopher/Shutterstock.com; p. 23 Purino/Shutterstock.com.

Printed in the United States of America

CPSIA compliance information: Batch #CS17GS: For further information contact Gareth Stevens, New York, New York at 1-800-542-2595.

Contents

Police officers
keep us safe.
They make people
follow laws.

Police come
to school.
They tell us how
to stay safe.

They helped Ann.
Ann was lost.
They found her mom!

POLICE
ONYX BARBERS
ONYX BARBERS

They helped Dan.
He was hurt.
They took him to a doctor.

Some police have dogs.
Police dogs can
find lost objects!

CAUTION
CAUTION

Police cars have
lights and sounds.
Here they come!

POLICE
POLICE

Some police ride horses in the park!

This is Officer Smith. She helps me cross the street.

POLICE

She rides a motorcycle!

POLICE

I can be a police officer.
So can you!

POLICE

Words to Know

motorcycle

officer

Index